# THE CAUTIONARY TALES OF CURIOUS SOULS

LIVVY HOLLIS

Book Cover and Interior Formatting by Livvy Hollis

Paperback ISBN: ISBN: 979-8-9881237-5-0

eBook ISBN: 979-8-9881237-6-7

First edition 2026

# CONTENTS

# A Note from Livvy

Dear Curious Readers,

I've always wanted to believe that magical beings exist hidden in the world around us. I want to embrace the stories of the faeries that paint the leaves in autumn and sprinkle their glittery dust on the snow. I want to believe friendly little gnomes really help my garden grow, and perhaps the little hummingbird that just buzzed by in blur was actually a curious little pixie that wanted a closer glimpse of me.

With that being said, if I'm willing to believe good, beautiful, and whimsical creatures like that are real, their less-friendly counterparts must surely exist as well.

If I'm going to leave honeyed bread out for the brownies, I'm also going to close my curtains as soon as it gets dark to hide from those who thrive under cover of nightfall. When I'm walking in the woods, I'll admire the beauty of the signs of the fair folk, but I'm certainly going to steer clear of their tricks and traps. Because I believe we can receive signs from loved ones long passed, I have to believe there are other things—beings with far less honorable intentions—beyond the veil that can reach through, too.

I could have written a collection of short stories showing the fun and joy that interactions with the magical world can bring. I could have given my characters their happy endings and went about my day. However, these characters won't be experiencing fairytale bliss.

This collection of six short stories shows what happens when everyday people, like you and I, encounter the more malevolent magical creatures that live among us. There are no happy endings and no warm, fuzzy feelings.

In today's world where everyone's looking for their handsome fae prince to whisk them away into a beautiful land beyond belief, I think it's important to remember there was once a time when people did everything they could to avoid such a fate.

Good luck out there.

—Livvy

# ONE

# As The Sun Rises

# ONE

Rosie Clark stepped into the rain, entering a sea of black. People sniffled and dabbed their tears with wadded tissues, their black umbrellas held high as they made their way down the hill following the casket.

Every red-rimmed eye was fixed on her as she made her way to the front of the procession. She smirked and fluffed the full skirt of the bright red dress she wore before finding a spot in the crowd beside her grandmother, who guided her in under the umbrella, although Rosie was already soaked to the bone. Her hair was plastered around her face, and beads of water clung to her unnecessary sunglasses, obscuring her vision.

As the priest began his readings, Grandma nudged Rosie's arm, a small smile on her lips. "Are you trying to kill your mother?"

"Not actively, no. Too many witnesses."

Rosie thought she heard a small chuckle escape Grandma's lips, but she kept her eyes on the casket being lowered slowly into the damp earth.

"She looks like she's about to have a stroke. You could have worn the black dress to appease her for half an hour, at least." Grandma's tone wasn't scolding but amused instead.

"Red was Grandpa's favorite color," Rosie whispered.

"And it looks fabulous on you." Grandma reached over to squeeze her hand.

"Grandma," she whispered, "I was thinking, and maybe I could stay with you for a bit. I'm done with classes for the semester and I don't start again for a while..." Rosie knew her request was partly selfish—she'd have done anything to avoid going home to her fun-fearing parents—but she also knew that Grandma hadn't been doing well alone these past few months now that Grandpa was...gone.

She refused to say or even think the word "dead." After all, that stupidly expensive casket they were burying was empty. They never found a body. Rosie believed that they never would because he was still alive. She could feel it; he just *had* to be. She just couldn't believe he could be gone without knowing it in her bones.

Grandma squeezed her hand even tighter. "I would love that."

She smiled in return and silently let a few tears fall. Between the raindrops on her cheeks and the sunglasses, no one would ever know.

A few days later Rosie was carrying the last of her boxes into Grandma's spare bedroom. She didn't have much, just clothing and books and other essentials. She decided to unpack quickly while Grandma finished lunch downstairs.

The ivory lace comforter on the bed was the same one that had been there nearly twenty years ago when Rosie had visited as a little girl. The lamp she'd broken when she was seven sat repaired, if a bit crooked, on the nightstand as it always had. The tiny nail holes still adorned the walls from when Rosie had convinced Grandma to let her hang string lights the summer she was twelve.

No matter how old she was or what was going on in her life, the consistency and comfort of her grandparents' home was always there. During the day, she and Grandpa would walk the trails of the forests behind their home, and in the evenings, Grandma would either craft or read while he worked in his carpentry shed.

Life there was always good. She felt a level of peace and love in their home that she'd never experienced anywhere else. And, although Rosie might be in her twenties now, that didn't stop Grandma from kissing her head and turning out her light before she shuffled off to her room for the night.

"Rosie," Grandma called from downstairs. "Lunch!"

Rosie smiled, although she couldn't help but feel strange at hearing Grandma only call her name. She was so used to hearing "Rosie, Jim, lunch!" called instead.

"I'm happy you're here, Rosie, really." Grandma smiled at her as she entered the room.

"I can hear the 'but' coming," Rosie hedged.

Grandma sighed, "But, now that you're in college, I'm surprised you don't have friends you'd rather spend your break with."

"Overrated," she said with a mouthful. "Really, I'd much rather be here with you."

"I'd hate to think you were giving up anything to be here watching over me. Rosie, I won't be around forever, you know, and—"

"Grandma"—Rosie set down her fork and looked in her eyes—"stop talking like that. I'm not resentfully *watching over you*. I'm happily and willingly staying with you."

She smiled sadly, and went back to eating quietly. After they finished their meals and took their plates to the sink, Rosie reached for her coat by the back door.

"I think I'm going to rake some leaves."

As Rosie raked, she couldn't stop the memories from flooding in: Grandpa raking a big pile for her to jump in and the two of them having leaf fights, tossing handfuls at each other, laughing.

She stopped, leaning on her rake, and stared at the forest. Tears threatened to fill her eyes, but she managed to keep them at bay. "There's no way," she whispered to herself, scanning her eyes through the red, orange, and yellow leaves that still clung to their branches. "You couldn't have just gotten lost out there, Grandpa. You know this forest better than anyone."

Her eyes landed on the carpentry shed that sat just beyond the treeline. It wasn't very big, but it was large enough to hold all of Grandpa's tools and machines. She made her way over, armed with her rake, to clear the pathway to the shed.

Even knowing he wouldn't be there, Rosie found herself peering through the windows hoping she was wrong. Everything inside was a bit dusty and disorganized. If Grandpa could see the neglected state of his favorite place, he'd be horrified. Imagining his dismay inspired her to clean the inside of the shed as well.

After retrieving the broom and cleaning supplies from inside the house, she slowly opened the shed door.

It creaked in protest but eventually gave way, stirring up dust as it hit the wall behind it. She started sweeping the sawdust on the floor and returning tools that were lying around to their designated places. Grandpa's unfinished project, a tall jewelry box for Grandma, lay on his workbench. He had just started to lay red velvet on the inside of the box but had not gotten a chance to finish the outer doors.

The bright, earthy smell of freshly cut wood filled the small shed. That scent had always lingered on Grandpa when he'd come inside and she'd brush sawdust from his white beard. The smell was still here, swirling around with the dust. She took a deep breath and sneezed.

She moved on to clean the windows, picking up the spray bottle and accidentally knocking over a slice of wood that clattered down to a larger pile of spare blocks on the ground. The pile fell apart then, blocks flying and scattering everywhere. Rosie staggered backward.

Her eyes darted around the room as a little red squirrel scurried from its ruined home and onto the workbench, where it stopped to look at her. Its little rib cage was expanding and contracting quickly, all four of its limbs spread out and ready to dart away if need be.

Rosie let out a shaky sigh, nervous that the squirrel might jump onto her, and whispered, "I'm sorry I scared you."

The squirrel sat up on its back legs. Its bushy red tail fluffed out behind it, and its tiny red ears twitched nervously.

"You can run away now," she told it. "I won't hurt you." She used the end of the broom to reach over and try to shoo it away. Instead, it jumped up onto the handle, perfectly balanced, and sat there.

"What are you doing, little one?" Her initial instinct told her to be cautious around wild animals but another piece of her—her animal-loving side, undoubetedly—was telling her that it was only as curious as she was.

Slowly, the squirrel made its way up the handle, and she tentatively reached out her other hand. It sniffed it, grasping her shaking finger with its little paw.

"Please don't bite me." Rosie smiled. "My fingers aren't food."

The little animal looked at her with its small black eyes for a moment longer before it scurried back down the broomstick to the work bench. There it sat, cleaning its twitching ears with its tiny hands.

"Well," she said as she moved slowly to pick up the spray bottle she'd dropped, her initial wariness fading away, "you can stay there if you'd like. I'm just going to clean the windows."

With the squirrel seemingly ignoring her, she began to clean one of the small windows at the back of the shed that looked out into the forest. Late afternoon sunlight illuminated the shed as she cleaned away the grime. Rosie peeked behind her, finding the squirrel was still there, watching her curiously.

"If you're still here tomorrow," she told it, "I'll bring you some breakfast."

The squirrel perked up and climbed the wall to run across a beam on the ceiling, jumping down on an old machine next to her. She chuckled, surprised by its tiny face that seemed so excited about a bit of food. Hesitantly, she reached her finger out toward it, hoping to pet its back. To her surprise, the squirrel stayed still, and she was able to slowly and gently run her fingers over its fur.

"You are such an odd little thing," she mused.

A movement of black outside the window caught her attention, and she gasped, spinning her head around and jerking her hand back. The squirrel, frightened by her sudden movement, was a blur in her peripheral vision as it disappeared further into the shed. When she went to investigate what she'd thought she'd seen, there was nothing there. She sighed, brushing off the feeling of being watched, and went back to cleaning.

That evening she went for a short walk, keeping to the usual trails and soaking in the golden sunlight that dappled through the leaves. The smell of earth and decaying leaves was a comfort to her. She and Grandpa had walked these trails countless times—their footsteps had worn the path in the dirt.

Reminded of his expertise in the forest, she kept telling herself there was no way he'd have gotten lost. If he had gotten hurt and couldn't call for help, that would be one thing, but then wouldn't his remains have been found?

Rosie cut her walk short as the sun began to set. It set earlier each night and rose later each morning during this time of year, meaning she'd have less time each day to search for him. As night fell and she snuggled into bed, she found herself staring out at the darkened forest. The moon was tucked behind thick autumn clouds. A gentle rain accompanied by a steady breeze made the trees tremble, sending their leaves tumbling to the ground.

Tomorrow she'd pack herself a lunch, bring a backpack of supplies, and spend most of the day searching the trails deeper in the woods. As her eyes fluttered closed for the night, she had a strong feeling that tomorrow she'd be successful. Tomorrow she would find out what happened to Grandpa.

Grandma had had a task lined up for the two of them to complete in the morning, which had cut into Rosie's searching time. Still, she was determined. She'd packed her bag and headed out into the woods around midday.

After Grandma's house dipped out of view behind her, Rosie soon noticed she was being followed. Her initial anxiety quickly dissipated as she looked up and saw the source of her worries. Gliding from branch to branch like an acrobat, a little squirrel was keeping pace with her.

She called up to it, "Are you the same little guy from yesterday?"

The squirrel did not answer, of course, but continued following above her, never going too far ahead or falling too far behind. It was nice to not feel alone on her search, even if her only companion was a little wild animal.

After she'd spent hours wandering the new trails she and Grandpa had mapped out, wondering if maybe there could be signs that he'd deviated from his planned route, she stopped to eat her lunch under a tree. The earth was still damp from last night's rain, but she didn't mind. As she bit into her sandwich, the little squirrel jumped down from the branches and sat in front of her, watching curiously. She threw some trail mix toward the little creature, and it began munching happily on the nuts and dried berries.

After her meal she noticed the sun was lower in the sky than she'd realized. She decided she would turn back soon, but she was so close to the end of her planned route. She hadn't been out this way before—it was a path she and Grandpa had planned to explore together.

The deeper she went, the older and more gnarled the trees became, their roots twisting up from the dirt like serpents, their branches so thick the fading sunlight barely reached the mossy floor. It was then, when she paused to take in her surroundings, feeling that something around her had shifted.

The air stilled, and the birds stopped singing. Rosie took a step backward, unsure if she should wait to see what would happen next or turn to head towards home.

The decision was made for her as a figure emerged from behind a large oak. It was a man whose contrasting features—grey hair framing a young face with wise eyes that still held the spark of a child—make it impossible to guess his age from his looks alone . His clothing was made of natural materials found there in the forest around them, and there was a sense of authority about him, as if the trees themselves bowed to him.

"You shouldn't have come this way, little girl," he said softly, but there was no threat in his tone, only an undeniable certainty.

"Who are you?" Rosie asked, curiosity momentarily overpowering the fear bubbling up within her.

The man plucked a leaf from the oak, twirling it between his fingers, and took a lazy step forward. His shadow moved alongside him as if it were its own seperate entity. It was impossibly dark and long, though it should have been near invisible as the sun settled below the horizon.

"Over the centuries I've had many names. Humans of every era used to worship me and bring me offerings right here below this very tree. Now, I've been forgotten, abandoned. No longer do they need the demigod in the forest to protect them from the predators. They've created their own weapons and left me to *rot*." As he said the words, the plump yellow leaf in his hand began to wilt and crumble.

"I'm only here because I'm looking for my grandfather," Rosie said, her voice shaking. Whether he was just a crazy man in the forest or something else older and evil, she wasn't sure. Still, she wasn't willing to risk not taking him seriously. "He's been missing for a while, and I thought he might have come out this way. I didn't mean to intrude on your space."

The demigod tilted his head. "Ah. But he's been by your side all along. Have you not noticed the little companion that follows you?"

As if on cue, the squirrel that had been traveling with Rosie leapt onto a low branch, chattering insistently. An instant later its body began to wobble, as if she were looking at it in a fun house mirror. Rosie's eyes widened as the tiny creature stretched and grew until finally Grandpa stood before her. He was just the same as he was the last day she saw him, though now there was a certain animalistic spirit about him

"Grandpa?" she whispered, barely believing her own eyes despite the events unfolding right in front of her.

"Rosie," he said, his voice hoarse. "Run! Get out of here!"

The demigod's gaze fell on Rosie. "Your dear old grandpa found me first, and, sadly for him, he could not pass my test. Now he remains with me, one of my forest's constant companions. Now, I offer you the same test, Rosie. Will you fail and join him, or will you prove yourself and earn your freedom?"

"What do you want from me?" Her voice shivered as the temperature dropped.

"If you can escape the forest before the sun rises, I will let you go."

Her heart beat faster, harder, its noise filling her ears as her panic surged. Rosie forced a deep breath. It was just after sunset, and though Rosie had been wandering for many hours, she was sure she knew this forest like the back of her hand. There should be plenty of time to make it back to Grandma's house before morning.

She had one chance. She could not fail.

"My grandpa, too." She managed to speak through her fear.

The demigod blinked as if surprised at Rosie's boldness. Then the mask of indifference was back on his face, and he shrugged. "Sure, why not? If you escape the forest before sunrise, you and your grandpa will go free. Now"—the demigod's smile widened—"begin."

Her legs burst into motion, running back the way she'd come. Whatever was left of her confidence slowly trickled away as she realized how different the forest was at night. Rocks and protruding roots were near invisible in the darkness, causing her to stumble. Branches she would have normally avoided seemed to jump out, reaching for her.

When she began to feel disoriented, she paused, wasting precious moments trying to remember all that Grandpa had passed on to her. He'd taught her how to follow moss patterns and navigate with the sun and stars and moon and wind. She could even start creating small markers—purposefully broken branches, perhaps—along the path to avoid going in circles. With another deep breath, she continued forward, a gentle prickle of hope grew inside her as she attempted to make use of her grandpa's teachings.

For a while, the strategies were working. Rosie was making progress, even beginning to see breaks in the trees, as if she were getting closer to the edge of the forest. She let out a sob of relief when she found a narrow trail that seemed familiar and continued down it. But then, to her utter devastation, it seemed the forest was coming alive. Trees shifted, their roots rising to block her way.

Distant laughter echoed. Rosie knew the demigod was watching, and he wasn't playing fair. What if there was no way for her to win? Perhaps he had no intention of letting her reach Grandma's house, after all. The heavy thought settled within her, weighing her down like a boulder.

Her mind raced: she had to move faster, think smarter. Minutes felt like hours as she dodged the wild trees. Her legs burned, her lungs ached, and as the first hint of sunlight began to lighten the sky to a gentle blue dawn, Rosie realized, with a sinking heart, that she wouldn't make it. She was lost, cold, exhausted, and outmatched.

Her mind shifted then to her grandma. She imagined her frail frame silhouetted by the kitchen light as she peered out the back door, worried that Rosie hadn't returned yet. And now she never would. Rosie may have found her grandpa, but could her grandma handle the inevitable heartbreak of burying another empty casket in a few months?

The demigod appeared before her, his form taking shape within a cloud of fog. She had no way of knowing exactly how much time had passed due to his tricks, but she could tell by the pale blue of the sky that the sun was creeping closer to the horizon. She had only minutes left.

The demigod's voice drifted toward her. "You tried, put forth a valiant effort. Nonetheless, it was not enough."

"Please," Rosie begged a final time, falling to her knees.

The fear finally stole her breath, her throat tightening. Her eyes widened in horror as the first slivers of sunlight pierced the sky. The world around her started to shimmer and wobble like heat rising off pavement in the summertime.

Her vision blurred as her body began to change. Her appendages shrank, her hands melting into tiny paws. Fur grew all along her body and a full, bushy tail sprouted behind her. Though the sensation was more uncomfortable than painful, she tried to scream, but only a high-pitched squeak escaped.

From the trees, her grandfather—back in the form of a small squirrel—chittered at her. It was no surprise that she could now understand what the squirrel was saying.

"Rosie, I'm so sorry."

The sun rose fully, spilling golden light across the ancient trees.

"You are clever," the demigod said softly, crouching so his face was closer to hers. "But cleverness alone cannot overcome the forest...or me."

Rosie skittered up the tree, overwhelmed by grief and defeat that seemed much too big for her new tiny body. She collapsed on the branch, burrowing her face in her grandfather's fur.

The demigod had disappeared, satisfied after having his fun. She sobbed harder, knowing this couldn't really be the end of his tricks. Surely, he would lie in wait for the next person to wander too far from the trail, too deep into the wood, too close to his trap. And, there was not a thing she could do about it.

Rosie only hoped Grandma wasn't the next curious soul to come searching.

TWO

With a
Final
Breath

# TWO

THE METAL DOOR OF the bar slammed shut behind Carter Jameson as he stepped into the alley. He pulled the lighter out of his pocket and lit the cigarette that hung from his lips. He sighed, huffing out his lungful of smoke and turned as the door opened again.

"Hey, man." His manager gave him an encouraging smile.

"Alex"—Carter took another drag—"that was rough tonight."

Alex sighed, leaning against the wall. "I know. But, I'm telling you, you're getting there, man. Your crowds are constantly tapping their feet and bobbin' their heads as you play that guitar of yours. And the way the girls swoon at your lyrics? You're the whole package, my friend."

An endless stream of cars zoomed out on the road at the other end of the alley while the crowds of people on the sidewalk kept their heads down as they walked. The alley smelled of piss and hot garbage, and Carter was unfazed by all of it.

"Then why does it feel like torture every time I get up there and play the same ten songs I've played since we started booking these shows?"

Carter had moved to the city with fifty bucks and his guitar in pursuit of his music career. He had a friend that had a cousin who knew a guy who said he could help get him started playing a few shows at some bars. That guy was Alex Cipriano, and he had kept his promises. Carter had started to climb the music scene ladder quickly under Alex's guidance, and soon Carter felt that his dreams were coming true.

Now here they were almost a year into their journey together, and Carter was questioning it all. The excitement he felt had begun to dwindle, and the monotony of playing the same few songs every night was beginning to feel like a chore. He'd tried to write new material, but he'd only managed to produce several garbage cans' worth of crumpled paper and empty cigarette packs.

"I think I know what you need, my friend." Alex clapped a hand on Carter's shoulder excitedly.

"I'm listening."

"You need a little break. A vacation. A retreat away from this city so you can get those lyrical juices flowing and write some new songs. That will help you find your joy again, guaranteed." When Carter looked at Alex skeptically, he added quickly, "Come on, have I ever led you wrong?"

Carter considered this, the idea of spending some time away quickly growing on him. "Where would I go? It's not like I have thousands to drop on a fancy hotel or anything." He flicked his finished cigarette onto the cement, grinding it into the ground with the bottom of his boot.

Alex pondered this for a moment, snapping his fingers as the idea came to him. "My uncle has this cabin up north. Real private, on a lake. I'm sure he'd let you stay there for a week or so."

This caught Carter's attention. "Seriously? That'd be amazing. Thanks, Alex."

"For you?" Alex jokingly punched Carter's arm. "Anything for you, my friend."

A few days later, when Carter's beat-up relic of a car pulled into the yard of the cabin, Carter felt lighter, eager to begin his vacation. He grabbed his duffel bag and guitar from the backseat. When he turned to walk toward the cabin, he couldn't help but stop for a moment to take in the scene before him.

Tall, thick evergreens lined the property, their shed needles carpeting the ground. The golden wood of the log cabin contrasted beautifully with the roof and door that were painted a deep red. Smoke billowed from the chimney—Alex's uncle must have been by to prepare the place for him—and a warm glow filtered through the windows. Perhaps most breathtaking of all was the lake that consumed the majority of the property. Wide and dark with gentle waves lapping the muddy shore, the lake was a gorgeous and welcome sight.

Carter knew that if he couldn't find inspiration here, he wouldn't find it anywhere.

Inside, the dry, warm air enveloped him. The cabin was sparsely decorated—a simple kitchen to the left, a wood stove with a crackling fire in the middle, and a cozy living space with a pull-out couch piled high with pillows and blankets. Alex had told him it would be a "rustic experience" but Carter was still disappointed to find the only toilet was an outhouse behind the cabin. At least there was a hand pump for water over the sink in the kitchen.

After settling himself by the fire, the icy stress he was carrying started to melt away. Alex was right, as he usually was; this was exactly wheat Carter needed. With a sigh of relief and an urge to write that he hadn't felt in a while, Carter unpacked his notebook and pen, grabbed his guitar, and began working out the fragments of a melody that had been fluttering in his head.

For three days Carter woke in the late morning, ate whatever he could find in the cupboards, and took his guitar out to sit on the bench by the lake. The simplicity was comforting, and the stillness of the lake—only interrupted by the occasional splash from a fish or ripple from a breeze—was steadying.

He strummed the strings on his instrument until his hand cramped, then stretched them out and wrote down the next portion of the lyrics as they came to him before picking up the guitar once again. This song would be something to be proud of, born of faded dreams reimagined and a passion reignited. Carter sang the chorus once more, as something still wasn't clicking properly.

"Sometimes I wish we could fall apart," he sang, "rebuild ourselves with the same heart..." He paused, the silence around him patient and understanding as he slowly continued, "on a foundation of memories, a place of..." Carter sighed, trying again. "A foundation of memories, a place of...loving...ease?"

He scratched the words down before he forgot them,

standing to stretch his legs and give his brain a break. He rested his guitar on the bench and lit a cigarette. The sun had set behind the trees, the blue filter of dusk tinting the world around him. Carter walked along the edge of the lake, humming his new tune, whispering the lyrics to himself.

When he heard his song being sung back to him from a mouth other than his own, Carter froze in his tracks, his eyes searching wildly for the owner of the feminine voice.

"Sometimes I wish we could fall apart"—the voice was in a higher key than his own, but complimented the melody he'd created perfectly—"rebuild ourselves with the same heart, on a foundation of memories, a place of loving ease." He ran back toward where he left his guitar, following the voice. It continued the lyrics past what he had come up with himself, singing, "A simple yet blissful melody I'll sing with each breath I dare to breathe."

Finally, he spotted her, a woman swimming in the water, smiling at him. He slowed his pace, coming to a stop a few feet away from the water's edge.

"How do you know that song?" he asked her.

"I've been listening to you." Her voice was as sweet as the forest air and musical in its own way.

"Where did you come from?" He looked around for another vehicle or perhaps another cabin. "Or, well, where do you live? I thought this cabin was the only one on this lake."

She giggled, diving under the water to swim closer to the shore. As she dipped beneath the water, a long, scaled tail emerged behind her, propelling her forward.

He blinked, disbelieving yet unable to look away. The waves coming across the water seemed to pulse in an ominous rhythm with his heartbeat.

Just when he thought she'd disappeared, she resurfaced, her smile revealing teeth that came to sharp points. A deeply embedded instinct told him to back away, to go back to the safety of the cabin. Instead, the woman started singing his song again, her voice overwhelming his thoughts.

Now that she was closer, Carter could see her more clearly in the dim evening light. Her long silky hair covered her breasts, and a few scales ran along her arms and dotted along her face like freckles. He was as frightened as he was fascinated. With a sense of caution mixed with curiosity, he grabbed his guitar and began to play his song from the beginning. He wanted to hear her voice again. He *needed* to hear it again.

His heart leapt as she began to sing, and he sang

with her, their voices merging for the perfect duet. He stepped forward. He needed to be closer. Another step. Closer.

The woman rose gracefully within the water, her hair falling like spilled ink. Her eyes met his, and the melody of her voice not only filled his ears but seemed to clutch as his heart. Every note spoke directly to his soul in a way no other music had before.

"Who...who are you?" he whispered.

She smiled but didn't answer him. Her tone lowered and slowed. She hummed a new, simple melody reminiscent of a lullaby a mother might sing to her restless child. Carter's feeling of curiosity began to fade as he listened, replaced with a sense of trust and longing that settled deep within him.

Carter took another step forward, feeling the slippery mud of the lake floor under his boots. He couldn't bring himself to care that his favorite boots were submerged or that the water was near freezing, not while she was singing, not while she beckoned.

"Come closer," she murmured. "Join me."

Deep within him, a voice—was it his own?—told him to back up, but the only voice that mattered in that moment was hers. He stepped farther into the water. The shock of the cold on his stomach made him gasp, and when the water reached his waist, he abandoned his guitar, which he left to float in the waves behind him.

The lake rose around Carter's chest, embracing him. His feet barely scraped the lake floor, but he continued forward.

Her hand reached toward him, and he obeyed her silent request, swimming until the water lapped at his neck and chin. His waterlogged jeans and jacket were weighing him down, his treading becoming more difficult as his muscles stiffened in the cold. When his hand finally brushed hers, an indescribable warmth and weightlessness overcame him.

Carter submerged with her, music still filling his ears as she sang under the water. She carried him deeper into the heart of the lake. Her song enveloped him even more completely than the water had, until the world above—the cabin, the city, his song—faded into nothing.

The stinging that was blooming in his lungs was difficult to ignore, and Carter tried to lift his hands, to reach for air, but the surface was invisible now, the darkness surrounding him. Bubbles tore their way free from his lips, traveling to the surface he had left behind.

Through the dark, murky water he caught one last glimpse of her, smiling sweetly at him with her razor teeth. With a final breath the lake water entered his lungs as the darkness pulled him fully under.

Above the water the world was silent—no singing, no music, no Carter, ever again. A well-loved guitar floated aimlessly along the waves, and a notebook, with lyrics to a song that would never be finished, sat on an otherwise empty bench overlooking the calm of the cold night.

# When the Fog Lifted

# THREE

THE MIST HAD ROLLED in thick that evening as Aiden Pierce kicked his soccer ball across the yard. He aimed between the makeshift goalposts he'd set up by shoving two sticks into the ground.

Aiden was in middle school now. He had to practice even harder if he wanted to be the best on his team. In elementary school it had been easy; everyone had just been trying to have fun together. Now, it was serious.

He set the ball down and jogged a few steps back, aligning himself perfectly. He darted forward, swinging his foot backward and then...

"Aiden! Come inside! Dinner's ready!" his mother called.

He flinched at the sound of her voice, his foot colliding with the ball in the wrong place. The soccer ball flew sideways through the air, completely missing his goalposts.

Aiden groaned, yelling back at his mother, "Just a minute, Mom!"

He followed his ball through the fog and into the trees at the edge of the yard. He sighed, frustrated. That would've been the best goal yet if she hadn't interrupted him. His mom always ruined everything.

She'd make his favorite dinner but then force him to eat the veggies first. She always made him turn off his video games when he was at the most important parts and never let him stay up past eight o'clock. When he'd had his friend Max over last week, his mother had embarrassed him so badly with a story from when Aiden was a baby, he couldn't even look Max in the eye the next day at school.

Probably the most annoying thing Aiden's mom did was keep his dad from coming over. He talked to his dad a few times on the phone a few times a week, but he lived somewhere else now with another lady. If his mom would just say sorry or invite him home or whatever, maybe his dad would come back to live with them and Aiden wouldn't have to only see him on the weekends.

As Aiden bent to pick up his ball, the mist swirling around his feet, he noticed something that definitely hadn't been there earlier: a cluster of mushrooms arranged in a perfect circle.

His ball temporarily forgotten, he knelt down, looking closer. The mushrooms looked similar to many other mushrooms, yet slightly different. They were quite large, some standing at least a foot from the ground. Some of them were held up by thick, cream-colored stems and had flat, wide, dark caps while others were smaller, with jelly-like tops and thinner stems. As his eyes adjusted to the dim evening light, he almost didn't believe what he was seeing. Tiny doors and windows had been carved into the stalks, glowing yellow lights illuminating the ground around them. He listened closely, as little voices and laughter drifted up from the circle.

Then, one of the mushroom doors opened. Aiden held his breath, watching as a tiny man stepped out. The little man was no taller than Aiden's hand and was dressed in earthy greens and browns. His cheeks were rounded and red, and he had a beard that was so long, it dragged on the ground.

The tiny person waved at him. Aiden blinked, sure he was imagining it, but then the man waved again.

"Hello," Aiden whispered, waving back.

The little man spoke, his voice high and squeaky like a cartoon mouse. "Hello! What brings you to our circle?"

Aiden didn't know how to answer but decided on a simple truth. "My ball rolled over this way. What's your name? I'm Aiden." As he spoke his name, he saw the little man's smile widen.

"Thank you for giving me your name. You may call

me Jotem. I am a gnome that lives in this circle."

"Why have I never seen you or this circle before?" Aiden wondered.

"We only appear when you need us. The circle knows your pain, dear Aiden."

"My...pain?" Aiden spoke slowly, confused at what the gnome's words meant.

"Your parents, your team, your struggles...the circle wants to make it all better."

"How can a bunch of mushrooms and gnomes make those things better?"

"Aiden." As Jotem spoke his name, a sense of calm washed over him, and Aiden realized he'd forgotten the question he'd just asked. He didn't need an answer anymore; an inner voice had appeared encouraging him to trust Jotem completely.

"If you wish to receive the circle's gift," the gnome said, "come back to the circle when the moon is at its peak."

Aiden's eyes widened, his heart beating faster with anticipation. He might not know what the gift was, but after Jotem had spoken his name and now continued to hold his gaze, Aiden felt that he wanted this gift more than anything. Whatever it was, it sounded better than pizza for dinner every night or video games until three in the morning. In that moment he knew he'd give up scoring the winning goal in his soccer game to get it. If he had the choice between this gift and living with his dad forever, he'd choose the gift. Hands down.

In a daze, Aiden stood and walked back toward his house. He ate dinner with his mother, politely answered her questions, and even finished his homework as she asked. She looked at him with a quiet curiosity, surely wondering what prompted his compliance, but Aiden couldn't bring himself to care. His mind was filled with the images of the gnome and the mushrooms and that mysterious, all-consuming gift.

When his mom tucked him in that night, he had no intention of sleeping. She kissed his forehead and flicked off his light, lingering in the doorway for a moment. "Aiden," she said, "I know things have been hard lately, but I want you to know I love you so much," she paused as if waiting for a response. When it didn't come, she sighed, "Sweet dreams."

He barely heard her.

Aiden stared out his bedroom window, watching as the moon rose agonizingly slowly. When it finally approached the top of its path, Aiden threw off his covers and tiptoed downstairs. His mother was asleep, and the house was dark. Normally he hated being alone in the middle of the night, but on this night he made his way to the back door and threw it open, not even bothering to put on his coat or shoes.

He ran barefoot across the dewy grass, the mist welcoming him like a pair of loving arms as he crossed the edge of the trees once more. The moon watched as the boy crept toward the mushroom circle, his heart pounding with excitement and fear.

This time, the mushrooms were fuller, a bit taller, and glowed an eerie blue light that covered the area around him. Only a breath later the gnomes appeared, smiling and happy and waving at him. He saw Jotem there and waved back at him.

"You came," one of the gnomes said. "Are you ready for the gift the circle promised?"

Aiden nodded, almost unable to speak. "Yes. I...I want it."

"Very well," another gnome chimed, raising a delicate hand. The blue glow of the mushrooms brightened. Aiden felt a tingling on his skin, and a strange weightlessness overcame him. He laughed, though part of him was still afraid. Slowly, he stepped into the center of the circle.

When nothing immediately happened, Aiden opened his mouth to ask Jotem what to do next. Before he could even take his next breath, Aiden's world swayed around him, the mushrooms began to grow taller, the little gnomes becoming more life-sized. It was only then that Aiden realized the circle and the mushrooms weren't growing—he was shrinking.

His arms and legs shortened, his fingers shrunk, and his clothes shrank with him.

A cheer rose from the gnomes that surrounded him as Aiden's body completed its transformation. He marveled at the new length of his hands; how could the gnomes have possibly made him so small so quickly, and how would they grow him back to his normal size?

Panic struck as his mind came back to him, Jotem's compulsion fading away. "Wait! I—you can change me back, right?" he squeaked, but his voice was high and strange, completely unfamiliar to his own ears. "This is really cool and all, but my mom can't wake up and find me like this. She'll totally freak out."

Jotem stepped forward. He was taller than Aiden now. "You have the spirit of a gnome," he said softly. "Untamable, wild, and ambitious. For this, the circle has gifted you a place among us. The circle is your home now."

"But..." Aiden shook his head, his heart nearly bursting from his chest as Jotem's words sunk in, "No, this isn't what I want! I want to go home!"

Jotem's tone lacked any sign of sympathy or understanding. It was cold and matter of fact as he said, "You may never return to the world beyond, though you will see much of it, as the circle never stays in one place for very long."

Aiden turned away, looking back at the faint outline of his house, barely visible through the mist. He caught sight of his soccer ball in the yard, though now it was nearly the size of a mountain. If he'd realized the last time he'd seen his team would be the *last* time, he would have played a bit longer with them. If only his dad had shown up that past weekend, then at least his final memory of him wouldn't be of him screaming at his mom.

That's when his heart really sank. His mom. When she woke up in the morning to his empty bed, she'd be in a panic; and he hadn't even said "I love you" back to her that night! The guilt and sadness that this thought brought felt as though it would crush him even if he'd been ten feet tall instead of ten inches.

As he'd predicted, shortly after the sun broke over the horizon, his mom ran wildly outside. She called for him, her voice trembling, darting around the yard. He'd tried to call back to her, his tiny voice too quiet and her sobs too loud. By the time the rising sun burnt away the fog, the mushrooms had vanished, and with them, Aiden had disappeared.

# The House That Kept Itself

# FOUR

Angie Williams sighed, enjoying the warmth of her driver's seat as the torrential downpour battered her car. She'd just pulled into the driveway of her new cabin—her fresh start, a chance to do it all right this time—and had been expecting the rain to have passed by now. Clearly mother nature was not on her side today. She wondered how quickly she'd be able to unload the trunk full of boxes and decided that even if she were the fastest woman in the world, there would still be no way to avoid getting soaked.

With a final sigh, Angie put up the hood of her jacket, popped her trunk, and jumped into the rain. The late autumn rain was ice cold, immediately chilling her to the bone. She ran to the cabin door, fumbling the key with shaky fingers until it finally slid into the lock and the door opened.

The small house came fully furnished, for which Angie was especially grateful. She'd left her husband—now ex-husband—taking with her only what she could fit in her car, which amounted to mostly clothing, a box or two of valuables, and other general essentials. She was sure there would be more she'd have to try to get back at a later date as she had truly rushed out as quickly as she could, but she knew she couldn't have stayed a minute longer with that lying, cheating, sorry excuse of a man.

Before diving back out into the downpour to retrieve her boxes, Angie shuffled over to the dark wood-burning stove—the only source of heat in the simple cabin. It had been years since she tried to start a fire, but she'd either succeed or get hypothermia. The previous owners had thoughtfully left some firewood and kindling, along with a box of matches, for her.

A handful of matches later, the fire just wouldn't catch. She rearranged the kindling and threw in another match with a grunt of frustration. Angie stood, telling herself she would just have to come back to it later and went to bring in a few boxes. When she returned, setting a dripping box on the floor, she was surprised but pleased to find a growing flame in the wood stove. Apparently her final attempt had been fruitful, after all.

When the last of the boxes was drying on her living room floor, Angie perched herself in front of the fire to warm up. She closed her eyes, soaking in the heat rolling off the flames and listening to their soft roar. The rain continued outside, and wind rustled the trees surrounding her new home. She was finally safe, warm, and alone. For the first time in weeks, Angie finally let a few tears fall.

Later that week when everything had been unpacked, their contents nestled into the new home, Angie had decided to make her first trip into town, which was several miles north. She thought she'd left her keys right on the table, but when she looked there was nothing but the vase with perky daisies. It felt like a good omen that the daisies were still looking fresh in the middle of November.

She didn't dwell on the thought long, as the hunt for her keys was still front and center in her mind. Angie rifled through the pockets of the coat hanging by the door, dug her hands through the couch cushions, and even glanced at the table a second time as she was sure that was where she'd set them. After tearing apart her room, searching under the furniture, and still coming up short, Angie was at a loss. She returned to the kitchen, and there, next to the vase of daisies, sat her car keys.

Angie slowly picked them up, unsure how she could have missed them the first two times she'd looked. Ultimately she was simply relieved to be able to continue on with her day. She shrugged it off and headed out the door.

The ride to town was peaceful and scenic. The temperature had dropped overnight, and instead of rain, little flurries of snow now fluttered down from the gray sky. As winter settled in and the roads became unpassable with snow and ice, Angie knew trips to town would be less frequent. With this in mind, she intended to stock up on as many groceries and other necessities as she could fit in her car.

Before heading to the grocery store, Angie decided to drop by the local cafe and warm up with a cup of coffee. While she waited for her order, a shaky voice came from over her shoulder.

"Is June's old house treating you well?"

Angie turned and blinked at the stooped elderly woman standing behind her. The woman's question had caught her off guard.

"I'm sorry, what was that?"

"You've just bought June Smythe's old cabin, haven't you?" The woman nudged her round glasses up on her nose. "Is it treating you well?"

Angie smiled politely. "It's certainly treating me better than my husband ever did!" When the old woman did not laugh, Angie cleared her throat and continued, "Mrs. Smythe's house is really lovely. It's warm and cozy, and I swear it keeps itself clean. I've yet to find a single cobweb, though I know the realtor said it had been vacant for several months. I think maybe my luck is finally looking up since I've moved here."

The old woman, bundled in several layers of sweaters and jackets, smiled politely. "You'd better thank your brownies."

Angie's eyebrows shot up in confusion. "Thank my what?"

"Brownies—little house elves. Helpful little things, most of the time. But if you don't acknowledge them or reward them for their efforts, the little buggers turn downright nasty."

"Uh-huh..." Angie turned to see if her order had been made yet, looking for any excuse to exit this conversation with the strange old woman. "I suppose I'm not familiar with...uh, brownies."

The woman nodded, pleased that Angie was at least somewhat receptive to her story. "I'm Bea, by the way."

"I'm Angie. Nice to meet you."

"Order for Angie!"

She grabbed her coffee, politely excusing herself as she eagerly raced toward the door. Bea's skeletal hand shot out, grabbing Angie by the arm, spinning her back around.

When Bea spoke again, her tone had turned dark. "You've done well not to anger them thus far, but that will not be enough forever. You must work to make them happy so you may continue to peacefully cohabit that home together."

"Excuse me," she said, trying to hide her annoyance as she tugged at the old woman's vice-like grip. "I really must be going."

"Sweet foods, shiny bobbles, a cup of cream—if you place them in the corner of the room, that'll do the trick."

Finally, Angie broke free of the old lady's grasp, backing away quickly.

As she yanked the door open, rushing out into the cold, Bea continued yelling at her, "Brownies or boggarts! Your choice!"

Angie shivered, partially from the cold but mostly from that odd encounter. Of course Angie would meet the town crazy lady on her first trip in. She sent up a silent prayer that she would avoid the senility that came with old age. It had to be hard having your mind slowly slip away.

The strange woman's words kept replaying in her

mind as she continued her planned shopping trip. By the end of the day, she found herself laughing at the whole thing, and eventually it was just another forgotten interaction.

That evening, after all of her purchases were put away, Angie was ready to relax. She grabbed the jug of milk she'd bought from the fridge; it was a bowl of cereal for dinner kind of night. She set the bowl on the table and turned to grab the box of cereal. When she turned back around, she noticed the daisies were finally starting to wilt.

Angie slid the window open and threw the browning flowers out onto the ground. The cold night air rushed inside as it tore its way through the forest. She shivered, quickly latching the window closed again. At least her home was warm and peaceful, and, most importantly, it was safe.

The spiders had clearly found their way through the cracks in the walls and into Angie's warm, dry home. She knew they were only trying to survive the winter, but they seemed intent on covering every inch of her home with their webs. She'd spent the better part of the morning dusting and decided to take a break to make a cup of tea.

Angie grabbed the milk she'd bought the day before to add a splash to her drink. When she took a sip, her face wrinkled in disgust, and she spit the tea out as quickly as she could. She twisted the lid off the milk again, and the stench that greeted her made it clear that the jug had gone bad, even though it had been fine for her cereal the night before. She examined the fresh-by date to be sure—it was over a week from today. If she hadn't been living alone, she would have assumed someone was playing a trick on her. Frustrated and confused, Angie dumped the rest of the jug down the drain and returned to cleaning.

She'd given the whole home a thorough scrub just a couple days ago, but looking at the state of her small storage closet, you wouldn't have been able to tell. Armed with her soapy bucket, gloves that came up past her elbows, and a trusty old rag, Angie began to scour the dirt and dust that had accumulated.

When she started scrubbing the back wall, a piece of the paneling shifted as if it had been loosened. Frowning, she set her bucket aside and pressed her palm to the loose board. The panel gave way, revealing a narrow, hidden space in the wall. Her frown deepened.

Inside the hollowed-out space was a nest; it seemed the spiders weren't the only small creatures to have found their way inside for the winter.

The nest had been constructed with scraps from what appeared to be old clothes, random bits of other soft material, and even dull strands of her red hair. Bits of cookies and candies were scattered throughout. What was particularly odd were the small trinkets that glittered among the mess. As she poked around in the pile, she found one of her earrings that had gone missing, as well as a spoon, a marble, a button that had fallen from her jacket the other day, and a penny. She added mousetraps to her mental grocery list and reached in, tearing the nest apart.

"Damn mice," she muttered, though she had never known mice to collect silverware and other odds and ends.

With the closet clean and her stomach rumbling, Angie went to change into a warmer sweater—no matter how large she built the fire, the winter chill was determined to stick around. She pulled open her dresser drawer and gasped at the shreds of sweaters before her. Angie slammed the drawer shut, wondering what kind of mutant mice had inhabited her home. To be able to build a nest that size so quickly and to so thoroughly shred her clothes, they had to be supernaturally en-hanced mice.

Angie paused. As she wondered about the little mice, Bea's words fluttered back into her mind.

*Sweet foods, shiny bobbles... Brownies or boggarts. Your choice.*

Angie shook her head, sending the thought away. If she started to believe in little elves that lived in her walls, soon she'd be just as crazy as Bea was. Still, the thought had somewhat rattled her.

Winter was digging in its claws and presented the first blizzard of the year that night. Angie grabbed every blanket in the house, stoked the fire, and curled up with a good book for the rest of the evening. When darkness had fallen over the forest, snow had piled itself against the cabin walls, and temperatures plummeted well below freezing, Angie decided it was time for bed.

She'd fallen asleep quickly but woke only a couple of hours later to a sharp pain in her foot. It had come untucked from the blankets and had been dangling over the mattress's edge. Angie flipped on her nightstand lamp and gasped at the sight of blood dripping onto her floor, pouring from a deep slash across the sole of her foot. She hissed, clutching it, her eyes scanning her bed, searching for a logical cause. Had she slid her foot across a broken piece of the metal frame or an exposed spring?

Surprisingly, everything was in its place. Whatever the culprit had been, Angie knew she had to stop the bleeding. Pulling on her robe, she limped to the bathroom. As she hobbled by, she noticed with annoyance that the fire had gone out in her wood stove—though there was no reason that it should have, she'd stocked it well—and her cabin was now black as the night around her.

She reached for the medicine cabinet in search of gauze and medical tape. Her fingers had barely brushed the mirror before the glass exploded, shards falling into the sink. Angie jumped back, her head whipping wildly around the room as she tried to make sense of what had happened.

Her breath trembled. Silence was all around her until a scratching came from behind the walls, as though dozens of unseen things scrambled within them.

Panic surged within her. She had no way of knowing what exactly was in the walls, but she was sure it wasn't mice and these creatures weren't going to leave her alone.

She fled to the living room, flicking on the light switch. The bulbs remained dark. The power was dead, whether from the storm or the creatures tormenting her, she didn't know.

Then chaos erupted.

Cupboards flew open and slammed shut. Plates and mugs launched into the air, smashing in all corners of the room. The dead fire roared back to life, flames leaping from the stove, sending up embers that sizzled as they landed on her skin.

The scream that had been building in her lungs finally tore free when her eyes fell on the tiny, darting shapes that moved in the shadows—too fast to see, too many to count.

Without a moment to think, she threw on her coat and slid her feet into her boots, grabbing her keys before darting out the door.

Outside, the storm had swallowed the world, the wind a howl that drowned all thought. Heart pounding in her ears, she found her way through the snow to her car, thrusting the keys in the ignition and turning them.

The car didn't respond—not even a click.

Angie curled in on herself, shivering, as she stared wide-eyed at the cabin door she'd left open, wishing she could go back inside. As if on cue, the door slammed shut, further cementing the fact that she was no longer welcome. She would just have to wait out the storm in her car. What else could she do?

The blizzard raged on. The cold became sinister, her fingers stinging, her breath coming out in puffs of steam. With a groan of frustration, Angie realized she couldn't go back inside but she couldn't wait here either. It was a choice between the unknown terrors in the cabin and freezing to death in her car. She considered attempting to walk to town, but she figured her chances of surviving ten miles through frozen darkness and knee-high snow were slim.

With a final burst of desperation, Angie climbed to her back seat. She kept a small hatchet, a can of pepper spray, a car window breaker, and a few other emergency items tucked away. She'd never expected she'd actually need them.

Half-frozen, Angie approached her cabin door armed with the hatchet and pepper spray. She reached for the handle, expecting it to be locked. Before her hand could grasp the metal, the door flew open with a bang. She hadn't a second to blink before she was dragged inside, her screams lost in the roar of the storm.

# Across The Lake

# FIVE

The house was quiet when Amelia Monroe's eyes slowly peeled open, as it always was. With her mother working an absurd number of hours as a hospital nurse and her father away on his second deployment, she was used to being alone. She'd see her mother for a few hours in the afternoon and on her occasional days off. Mostly, Amelia didn't mind being by herself.

Bright yellow morning light filtered through the trees outside her window. In that groggy space between waking and sleeping, everything was calm and peaceful. If only it would last.

A glint of light reflected off the glass of a new picture frame, catching her eye. Her brand-new high school diploma was displayed in that frame. She knew she should be able to look at it and feel a sense of pride in her accomplishments and an eagerness to move forward after graduating, but for Amelia the future was still so uncertain.

She groaned, rolling out of bed. As she ventured into the kitchen in search of coffee—assuming her mother left her some—Amelia noticed a note taped to the cupboard. She could almost hear her mother's overly cheerful tone as she read her cursive scrawl.

*Amelia,*

*I only work half of a shift today—covering for Sarah. I'll be home at 2. Someone bought the Smiths' old house across the lake, and I'd like us to be good neighbors and bring them a welcome treat! Grandma Bonnie's apple pie recipe is on the back of this note. Please be helpful and get it made before I get home. Love you!*

*—Mom*

Her eyes rolled so hard in her head she could nearly hear them rattle. She wasn't about to spend this gorgeous summer day baking a pie for some neighbors she would never see or care about. She would still satisfy her mother's request, of course, but in a different way.

Amelia took a few minutes to brush her hair and get dressed before grabbing her phone and wallet and stepping out the door. She walked around the side of her home, sighing as she glanced at her broken-down car. She hopped on her bike and started down the dirt path that would take her around the lake and onto the main paved road that led to town.

A moving van was positioned outside the only other home on the lake. The van door was wide open, and a few small pieces of furniture were still inside. The neighbors were nowhere to be seen. She couldn't help but stare, hoping for a glimpse of the newcomers. When her bike hit a large stone nearly sending her down the hillside and into the lake, she decided to keep her gaze positioned in front of her.

The ride to town was less than an hour long. With the sweet summer breeze, chirping birds, and lush greenery, it was peaceful, too. With a gentle smile on her face, Amelia gave her pedals a final few turns before coasting gracefully into the grocery store parking lot.

Inside she secured a frozen apple pie and a soda for herself. She paid, smiling sweetly at the cashier. Thankfully the pie box and soda fit perfectly in her bike's basket, if it hadn't that would have made for a much more annoying ride back. Satisfied with her purchase, Amelia made her way home.

When the pie was baking in the oven, the box shredded and buried in the trash, Amelia perched herself on the edge of the dock with her feet dangling in the lake. She pulled out her cell phone and called her best friend—her confidant, her cheerleader, her favorite person—Jess.

"Hey, Jess, whatcha up to?"

"Hey! I'm just packing my things," Jess sighed. "I still can't believe you're not going to be at college with me! We haven't been apart for this long in, like, ever!"

Amelia picked at her thumbnail nervously, "I know, I know. I just..." She couldn't find the right words to explain her plans. This was partly because she didn't *have* any plans, but also because a part of her wanted to find something exhilarating, something life-changing!

"Have you made any decisions about what you're doing next?"

"Not really," Amelia answered honestly. "I might just take a gap year, you know? Life is so short, and I've spent the majority of mine in school already. I think it'd do me well to travel, enjoy my freedom."

"If I took a gap year"—boxes shuffled in the background as Jess continued packing—"I'd never want to go back to school."

Little fish swam around Amelia's feet, carefree and calm. She grasped for a way to change the subject.

"So, I guess we aren't the only occupants of Lynden Lake anymore. Apparently someone bought the Smiths' old house." She glanced up as the movers closed the van and hopped in the cab, ready to drive off.

Jess took the hint. "Oh yeah? Could be a handsome man, ready to go with you on that gap year of yours."

Amelia scoffed, "Oh, be serious. It's probably just some old retired couple looking for a quiet place to live out their final years. Mom asked me to bake a pie as a welcome gift for whoever it is. We're going over there later."

"Sounds fun." Her tone dripped with sarcasm, "Hey, let me call you back tonight. I've got to take these boxes down to the car. Talk to you later!"

Amelia was able to whisper a single goodbye before the line clicked. She stared at the house across the lake for a moment, hoping to catch a glance of the new neighbors, when she heard the kitchen timer faintly buzzing inside.

She ran inside, pulling the pie out of the oven before digging through the cupboard for a glass pie dish. She transferred the pastry to the glass dish, hoping she could pass it off as homemade.

There was only an hour left until her mother got home, which gave her just enough time to finish her hair and makeup. The time passed quickly, and as she finished taming her frizzy hair she heard the front door close.

"Amelia?" her mother called.

"I'll be down in a moment!"

Amelia entered the kitchen to find her mom inspecting the pie. She held her breath, waiting to see if her ruse would be discovered.

"It smells delicious, darling!" Her mother kissed her

forehead as she walked past. "Give me a moment to change out of these scrubs then we can head on over. After this, I'm putting on my jammies, and my butt is *not* leaving the couch."

Amelia smiled, grabbing a handful of forks and a stack of paper plates from a drawer, in case the neighbors hadn't unpacked their kitchen boxes yet.

When her mother returned, grabbing the pie, Amelia followed her out the door with the forks and plates. Together they crossed the short grassy path that led around the small lake and to the dingy old house.

After a quick succession of knocks on the door, Amelia and her mother waited only a few seconds before the door swung open. A boy who, at first glance, appeared to be around Amelia's age, stood there with a careful smile on his mouth. He was tall and thin, his skin pale and eyes dark.

"Hello," he said, voice soft, almost melodic. He tilted his head like a curious cat, appraising her with an intense focus that sent an odd chill down her spine.

"Hello!" her mother said brightly. As she dove into the explanation of their visit, Amelia looked curiously past the boy into the home.

Behind him, two adults paused mid-movement. Immediately it was obvious there was something not quite right about them. Their skin was dull, almost waxy, and though they were clearly young—maybe late twenties—their posture held an air of frailty. Their eyes flicked toward her, but there was no warmth or curiosity in their gaze, only a calm indifference. They returned to unpacking silently, their movements slow, almost rehearsed.

"Please," the boy said, stepping aside and bringing Amelia out of her thoughts, "come in."

As they gathered in what appeared to be the future living room—though for now it was covered in stacks of boxes and only a simple set of two couches in the middle—the boy continued speaking.

"I'm Will. This is my mother, Jane, and my father, Stephen."

So they were his parents; Amelia wondered how young they must have been when they had him but didn't have time to linger on the thought.

"I'm Brandy and this is my daughter, Amelia." Her mother handed her the pie, feigning a sense of normalcy though Amelia knew her mother well enough to see that she also felt something was not quite right here. "Amelia, dear, would you cut us all a slice?"

"I'll show you where the kitchen is," Will offered, his tone flat.

Amelia nodded, following him. They stepped inside the small room and she moved to set the pie on the counter, using the spatula to cut and serve slices on the paper plates. Will was hovering in the corner, watching silently. As she went to plate the last piece, he stopped her.

"None for me, thank you."

She nodded once. The silence that returned to the small space they shared was nearly overwhelming.

"So, are you excited to be living by a lake?" she asked, grasping for normal conversation. "It's wonderful in the hot summer months, and you won't believe the sounds the lake ice makes in the winter."

He turned to her, his dark eyes glinting. "Yes, I'm looking forward to being here. It's...quiet," he said and then added, almost as an afterthought, "Secluded. We value our privacy quite a lot."

Amelia laughed nervously. Something about the way he said that had almost sounded like a threat, though she couldn't figure out why that might be. She brushed it off, smiling politely, and handed him a couple of plates to carry into the other room.

Her mother sat awkwardly on one couch as his parents sat rigidly on the other. She looked relieved when Amelia walked in, sighing and scooting over to make room.

"Amelia, Will's parents just mentioned they moved here from Colorado! I was telling them that's one of our bucket list destinations."

Will went to stand behind his parents, who were holding their plates on their laps, staring in an almost confused way at the pie in front of them.

Amelia took her place next to her mother and began to eat quickly. This family was giving off the strangest vibes, and the faster she finished her food, the sooner they could leave. Her mother seemed to have the same idea, chattering out a few words of small talk between bites.

Will answered all of her mother's questions, his parents shifting their blank stares from their plates to random places in the room, looking at nothing in particular. Amelia couldn't take her eyes off them. There was something in the way they barely moved or breathed, or even blinked, that made her stomach tighten. Curiosity flared alongside a budding fear. She wanted to ask if everything was okay with them, but between her instinct and general politeness, she held her tongue.

Her mother, seeing that Stephen and Jane hadn't touched their food, announced that she didn't want to take up too much of their time and that she would stop by on another day to pick up her pie dish and utensils. With an awkward wave goodbye, Amelia and her mother nearly ran out the front door.

When the door closed behind them, Amelia turned to her mother. "Well, they were..."

"Strange," her mother chuckled, finishing the thought.

Although her mother's agreement made her feel at ease, Amelia found herself glancing over her shoulder. Will was standing in the window, his eyes still on her. For a moment she could have sworn there was a deep anger—or maybe it was a sadness—she didn't seem to understand.

The next day Amelia found herself glancing out the windows toward Will's house every few minutes. Not once did she see any signs of life—not a single light turned on, a curtain shifted or a window opened. She tried to distract herself in every way imaginable, but she couldn't stop thinking about them.

Perhaps it was the way Will moved, as if he were gliding from room to room. Or maybe it was the unnatural stillness and overall haggard appearance of his parents.

Whatever it was, the memory of their ten-minute encounter gnawed at her all day. By nightfall, she found herself creeping toward their house, an insatiable need to know more propelling her forward.

She kept to the shadows along the lake's edge as the light from the full moon shimmered on the water. Each step made her heart pound like a drum. Her shoes sank slightly into the damp earth, and the air smelled faintly of fish and rain. She'd often take walks around the lake at night, finding them peaceful. Tonight was nothing like that.

When she made it up to the window, she peered inside, her fingers gripping the sill and her head barely popping up over the edge. Will's parents were as still as the couch they sat on. For a moment she wondered what they were doing there, staring blankly into the distance. The TV was off, and there was no music playing or books in their laps. Amelia was about to step away when Will crept in from the back room. His movements were smooth and graceful, like a cat stalking its prey.

He came up behind his father and bent forward, as if to whisper something in his ear. Then he leaned a bit further in, his mouth brushing against his father's neck.

Her stomach churned nervously, but her legs refused to move. At first, Amelia couldn't figure out what she was seeing. Perhaps she didn't want to accept what was right in front of her.

The boy stood only a moment later and threw his head back, sighing deeply. His mouth was a sickly red, stained by the blood that slid down his father's neck from two open puncture wounds.

A wave of dread washed over her. Internally she cursed her curiosity—if only she'd stayed in bed. She began to back away, wanting nothing more than to run inside her home, lock her door behind her, and forget everything she'd seen.

A twig cracked under her foot. She froze with nowhere to hide, her eyes locked on the window in front of her.

The boy's head snapped toward her, blood dripping from his chin. He didn't move, didn't even blink, but she felt the weight of his stare. To her growing dismay, his lips turned up in a predatory grin.

Before she could react he leapt forward with impossible speed. He was opening the window one moment and the next he was standing there beside her, his gaze piercing into her with a force that stole her breath. Amelia tried to scream, to run, but her fear kept her locked in place.

"Curious," he said, his voice low, almost playful, yet edged with danger. "Usually humans' instincts tell them to stay away from me, still here you are for a second time in two days."

"I...I'm sorry," her voice was almost unrecognizable to her own ears, "I'll just go home, and I won't say a word about any of this."

"I know." He grabbed her arms with his vice-like hands. "I know you won't be saying anything."

She couldn't move, couldn't breathe when he leaned in as if to kiss her jaw. A hot sharp pain spread along her neck but was slowly replaced by a cool numbness. Amelia's heart was beating harder than ever before, trying to circulate blood that was no longer in her veins.

Thoughts raced through her mind. Suddenly Amelia knew she wanted to go to school with Jess. She wanted the dorm and the classes and the parties. She pictured the day her father would be home for good and her mother would take on less hours at work. They'd spend holidays together, visit her at school, maybe even meet her future partner... She wondered if she had just called her friend instead of sneaking outside tonight, if that life might have been possible.

Her vision began to blur, and her world began to

spin. She knew what this meant: her brain lacked the blood it needed to function.

A final question fluttered through her mind as he drained her body: what would he do with her body? Would her mother find her there, stiff and cold in the mud? Maybe he'd make it seem as if she'd disappeared completely—ran away in the night, never to be seen again.

Words bubbled up inside her, but she couldn't speak. She wanted to make a final request, to ask that he spare her mother. Too soon, the darkness began to creep in, and her eyes fluttered closed.

The lake behind them was still, the moon's light bright and oddly serene. The only sound to be heard was the crunch of gravel as Amelia's mother pulled into the driveway of their house. As it all faded into nothingness, Amelia's body went limp, and she collapsed in her killer's arms.

SIX

# A Tide Turned

# SIX

FOR THE LAST FIFTEEN years, Erin Wilkes had been dedicated—though some might say obsessed—to her studies and her career. She'd always been ambitious and intelligent, so when she decided to go to law school, no one was surprised.

When she graduated top of her class and secured one of the most coveted internships in the industry, no one batted an eye. So, when she was on track to becoming the youngest partner at her firm, everyone said they had seen it coming. Through it all she still managed to maintain a relationship with one of the most eligible bachelors in the city—well, until he slept with an intern and she left him high and dry.

Erin always set the bar high and then jumped higher. She achieved every goal, set every precedent, yet still at the end of each day she felt unfulfilled. She had spent so much time chasing, growing, climbing the ladders set before her, that she never stopped to ask herself if doing so was actually bringing her joy.

When she realized she couldn't remember the last time she'd experienced a truly joyful moment, Erin quit her job. She then sold her home, liquidated all of her assets, and moved to a remote seaside town where she bought a small bungalow.

She'd been there about a month and still felt like an outsider in the small town. A few dozen families lived in the village, and the majority of them had descended from the families that had been there since the land was settled a few hundred years ago.

Still, Erin was happy to have found the little town by the sea. Despite the gossipy locals and the near-constant cover of rain, she really felt she could make a life there. She had been the subject of their gossip and had endured their whispers and sideways glances, but the person they seemed to talk about the most was a little old woman who lived in a small cottage on a cliff by the seaside.

They called her Muriel Harlow or, more commonly, "the sea witch." Everyone insisted she was harmless despite the foreboding nickname they'd given her. Erin heard that Muriel had lived there forever, yet no one was quite sure how old she was. Some said they remembered her as a young woman, but others claimed she was old even a few decades ago. Erin couldn't help but chuckle at the stories and rumors.

Without ever meeting Muriel, Erin felt a kinship to this reclusive outsider, as Erin had been branded much the same by the locals. One afternoon, she made a batch of cookies—baking was a hobby she'd been trying out, and she was finally getting the hang of it—and decided to take a walk to Muriel's home. Maybe the old woman was feeling just as lonely as she was.

Erin knocked on the door, plate of cookies in hand. In the moment between knocking and waiting for the door to open, a strange sense of nervousness began to creep up inside of her. She debated turning and going back home when the door creaked open, revealing a short, hunched-over woman, Erin stood frozen, a polite smile on her face.

"Ah, yes, Erin," Muriel said. "I was wondering when you'd come by to visit me."

Erin blinked. "Excuse me?"

Muriel laughed, "I heard your name when I listened in on some women's conversation in the grocery store. I thought you might introduce yourself one day."

"Right." Erin was still skeptical but did her best to brush off the feeling. She held out the plate in front of her. "Well, I brought you some oatmeal raisin cookies."

Muriel stepped aside, her waist-length gray hair swinging behind her. "Please, come in out of the cold."

Erin took a step forward. When she was inside the cottage, she immediately felt warm to her core, the smell of salt and sage filling her nose. Muriel took the plate of cookies to the modest two-person table in the corner by the large hearth fire. Erin followed, her eyes taking in the small space.

The room was cozy, homey, though filled with strange things. On the shelves, jars of sea water caught the light, little bits of shell and seaweed floating inside of them. Between the jars sat pieces of driftwood and long white sticks that were polished smooth, as though they had been worn by the ocean waves—though they looked suspiciously like human bones. Most peculiarly, along the far wall hung a dozen clocks all ticking out of sync and a dozen more mirrors, some tarnished and dull.

"Tea?" Muriel offered. "You look like you may be in need of a bit of grounding, dear."

"You really are a witch, aren't you?" The words spilled from Erin's lips before she could stop them. Perhaps her tongue was so loose because what she felt was a calm curiosity, not fear or anxiety.

Muriel only chuckled, "Guilty as charged. Though, I'm not like the witches in fairy tales, I can assure you. Now, dear"—she set the tea in front of Erin—"what's upsetting you?"

For some reason, Erin's confession was eager to come

out. She sighed and took a sip of her tea. "I moved here because I felt lost, and now I'm unsure what comes next."

Muriel nodded gently. "The world rarely tells women what comes next after they've finished surviving and try to truly live."

Erin felt tears prickle her eyes. "Exactly. I thought I was on the right path my whole life, that I was thriving. But I couldn't have been more wrong. I was just doing what was expected of me."

Their conversation continued for a short while. Muriel comforted Erin and Erin shared more with Muriel than she'd ever expected she would share with a perfect stranger. There was just something about the old woman that drew Erin in.

The gentle sound of the waves lapped in the background, until the sun began to set. Erin politely excused herself, feeling lighter and more hopeful. She promised Muriel she would return again the next day.

Over the following weeks, Erin visited often. Muriel had become the lighthouse on the foggy path Erin had set herself down. She believed it was fate that the two of them met and she was especially grateful when Muriel decided to teach her a few witchy things.

When Erin was having stress nightmares left over from her rigorous career, Muriel showed her how to gather the sea water during the full moon, boil it away until the salt was left behind, then sprinkle that salt under her pillow. Just like that, the dreams stopped. She learned how to read meaning in seabird flight and was then able to accurately predict when storms would roll in over the water.

The lessons felt *good*. They made Erin feel powerful, like she was reclaiming herself after far too long. She was beginning to feel whole; pieces she hadn't even known were missing were starting to fall into place. She even started to paint again, something she hadn't done in years.

Erin sat by the fire in Muriel's cottage, warming her hands after spending the afternoon collecting seashells with Muriel along the beach. Muriel was making tea, as she often did, and was muttering to herself. Erin could barely make out what she was saying, but heard a few words flutter from the kitchen: "She's nearly ready."

"Ready for what?" Erin asked.

Muriel smiled sweetly. "For the tide to turn."

Erin stood, perusing the small selection of books

on the bookshelf while she waited for the tea. One, a plain leather journal with nothing written on its cover, called out to her. She grabbed it, gently turning its thin, yellowed pages.

It appeared to be filled with a list of names and dates; the entries spanned many decades though they were all written in the same steady hand. Each section ended with a name crossed out and a new one written beneath it. Each name, she realized, was another woman: Mary Jones, Elizabeth Barton, Henrietta Bordeau, Janet Paulson... The list seemed never-ending.

On the most recent page, the last name that was crossed out was intensely familiar: Muriel Harlow. More terrifying than that, there was a name written below Muriel's.

Erin Wilkes.

"What is this, Muriel?" Erin stormed into the kitchen, confused and scared. She shook the journal in her hand. "Who were all these women in the journal, and why have you written my name?"

Muriel didn't try to deny or deflect anything. She remained calm as she finished the tea. The seconds grew heavier as they passed, the ticking of the clocks on the wall sounding like drumbeats. Still, Muriel remained silent, even as the flames in the hearth began to flicker wildly, sending green sparks into the air.

"Muriel!" Erin could hear her voice trembling. "Answer me!"

"You've felt it, haven't you?" Muriel spoke without turning. "The pull of the tide, the hum in your bones? The sea has chosen you, same as it chose me."

Erin took a stumbling step backward. "What does that even mean?"

"When I was your age, I stood on that shore and begged it for a place in the world. I was tired of being small and frightened, so I promised the sea my service. In return, it gave me time...too much of it. But nothing comes for free." Muriel turned, a deep sadness in her eyes. "Magic doesn't stay still; it needs a vessel to hold it. But when that vessel's body grows old, the magic must pass on, or the sea grows restless. So every few decades, it sends me someone to use to replenish my energy."

"Is that all I am?" Erin's legs shook, her heart raced.

"Oh, no, dear. This time, I don't want to be restored. I want to rest. I've been the sea's servant long enough." She smiled softly. "It's true that when you came to me, at first I thought the sea had sent you as another energy source. Then I saw you had the same ache I once had, a similar hunger for meaning. The sea heard you, too, Erin. It chose you to be my successor before you ever knocked on my door."

Erin shook her head wildly, stepping back again, inching closer to the door. Toward freedom and away from the sea witch. "No. No, I don't want this—to be trapped here in this place, feeding on innocent people. You used me!"

The cold weight of betrayal washed over her. Had any part of her friendship with Muriel been real? After everything Erin had shared with the old woman, had Muriel even once considered all that she was robbing Erin of? She'd just begun feeling alive again after so long of simply existing. What kind of life would she have to endure now, cursed by a power much larger than she ever was?

"No, my dear." Muriel gently shook her head, "I *freed* you. You wanted a place in the world, and now you'll have one, here, by the sea."

Erin tried to run, throwing open the door and tearing down the path. The sea had no intention of letting her escape, though, and began to churn wildly, its waves flooding the land and bringing Erin to her knees. She looked back as the cottage began to flood, but it made no difference. Something terrible was already in motion.

The old woman's body began to fade. She dissipated like mist rolling off the sea before condensing once again and reappearing at the edge of the cliffside, arms outstretched wide. Her voice echoed beyond the waves and across the seaside hills, carried by the gale that came in over the water. "You said you wanted a new life, my sweet. I'm giving it to you."

The waves grew more intense, soaking Erin and filling her lungs. She spewed sea water, coughing and choking, when suddenly the storm cleared, the waves receding back to their origin and taking Muriel with them.

Erin tried to stand, to move back toward her home, but her legs wouldn't go any farther, as if an invisible barrier wouldn't allow her to move too far from the sea. Tears streaming down her face, Erin turned to see the witch's cottage standing miraculously untouched as though it hadn't been submerged only moments ago. She trudged back toward her only shelter, defeated and trapped.

As the newest caretaker of the sea's magic, Erin could hear whispers—that had once only sounded like the simple splash of the water—roll in on the waves. She knew the sea spoke true as it told her she could never leave this place. She was now bound to the sea itself, tasked to contain its magic for many lifetimes to come, and the sea didn't take no for an answer.

Somewhere deep below the tide, in the cold dark water, Muriel finally slept, her rest well-earned after lifetimes of servitude.

# About the Author

Livvy Hollis is a proud independent author with a life-long love for fantasy and romance. She published her first novel at twenty-five, but her passion for storytelling began in childhood, inspired by the enchanting tales her grandmother shared and the magical beauty of her home state of Michigan.

She writes stories about people finding their place in the world and the magic that happens along the way. Her books offer readers an escape into enchanting realms filled with immersive magic, fantastical creatures, and exciting adventure.

For Livvy, writing is both a calling and a refuge—a way to keep love and magic alive in a world that can sometimes feel too heavy. She plans to continue writing stories as long as her fingers can dance across a keyboard.

You can find Livvy on Facebook, Instagram, Threads, and TikTok, or join her newsletter at www

.livvyhollisbooks.com to be the first to hear about new projects, giveaways, and more.

# ALSO BY

# LIVVY HOLLIS